"For Turnip, Carrot, and Puchu -
the rescued cats and dog who in turn rescued me."
- *Aparna Karthikeyan*

"For my son Juri."
- *Christine Kastl*

Aparna Karthikeyan is an independent journalist.
She documents rural livelihoods in Tamil Nadu
and volunteers with People's Archive of Rural India.
She is working on books of short fiction for children
and non-fiction for adults. She lives in Mumbai with
her husband, daughter and dog.

Christine Kastl grew up in Germany. She studied art and
design in Germany and illustration in Strasbourg (France)
at the ESAD (Ecole Supérieure des Arts Décoratifs). In 2007,
she was awarded the Kunstförderpreis Friedrichshafen,
a prestigious art award.

Cat's Egg

© and ℗ 2019 Karadi Tales Company Pvt. Ltd.

Text: Aparna Karthikeyan
Illustrations: Christine Kastl

Karadi Tales Company Pvt. Ltd.
3A Dev Regency,
11 First Main Road,
Gandhinagar, Adyar,
Chennai 600020
Tel.: +91-44-4205 4243
email: contact@karaditales.com
www.karaditales.com

ISBN: 978-81-9365-422-4

Printed and bound in India by
Manipal Technologies Limited, Manipal

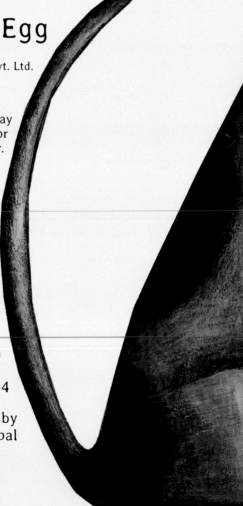

Cat's Egg

Aparna Karthikeyan | Christine Kastl

"Woof, woof!"

"Quiet there," says Cat. "I'm hatching a kitten."

Dog looks surprised. "But..." he says politely,
"that's not how it works."

"What do you know?" scoffs Cat.
"You're a dog."

"Did you lay it?" Dog asks, when Cat
stretches and he sees underneath her tail,
a golden egg.

"I found it this morning when I woke up.
I must have laid it in my sleep," Cat says,
looking fondly at the egg. "Isn't it the
exact same shade as my fur?"

Dog shrugs. The egg seems a pale shade
of yellow. Cat's fur is bright orange.

Dog sits next to her basket.

"How long does it take to hatch a kitten?" he asks.

"Oh, three days at least," Cat says.

"Isn't that very quick?" Dog wonders. "Baby crows take eighteen days."

"Oh!" Cat says, pretending not to be surprised, and adds quickly
as she walks away, "Listen, sit on my egg for a bit. I will be back
after a little lunch."

Dog looks at the egg for a full minute.
He runs after Cat.

"I don't know how to do this," he pants,
"you need someone with experience. Ask Crow!"

"You are so useless," Cat says, and carefully
picks up the egg in her mouth.

She walks to the garden and mewls beneath the tree.

"Go away, Cat," Crow caws.

"I need help," Cat purrs, placing the egg carefully between her paws.
"I want you to watch my egg."

"A cat egg? That's a first," Crow says, peering at the egg.

"Please mind the egg, won't you? I need a snack and some sleep,"
Cat says and starts to walk away.

"Hey, come back! There's no room in my nest,"
Crow squawks. "Besides, all mine are blue and big.
Yours is small and yellow. I can't take it in!"

"Blue eggs and black feathers, ha!" Cat sneers,
picks up the egg and stalks off.

The evening sun blazes. Cat is annoyed.
She is peckish. Sleep plucks at her eyes
and she feels a catnap coming.

She hears Cuckoo singing. She places
the egg on the warm ground.

"Care to watch my egg for me?" asks Cat.

Cuckoo whispers, "I wouldn't know how. I lay mine in Crow's nest.
Two over there," she points at Crow's nest, "are mine."

"Won't she find out?" Cat asks.

Cuckoo shrugs and coos, "All of us were
raised by crows."

Suddenly Cat remembers the beach Turtle
planning a family. She picks up the egg –
now hot and a little soft – and leaps over
the garden wall.

"Turtle," Cat says, "I have a surprise for you."

"What is it?" Turtle asks.

Cat gently rolls the egg forward.
"Please keep it with yours," she purrs.

"I bury mine," Turtle says, "and go back to the sea."

"I'll come by in three days and pick up the kitten," Cat offers.

"Hmm," Turtle says, "but your egg smells."

"Rubbish!" Cat snaps, "my egg is perfectly lovely."

"And it's gone all damp," Turtle points.

Cat picks up the soggy egg and rushes
back home.

"Dog!" Cat wails, waking up sleeping Dog.
"Dog, my egg is destroyed."

Dog sniffs the egg; he pokes the damp bits.
It peels away, and underneath, it's gooey and
oozy and looks like it is melting.

"Cat, this is an Easter Egg. It's a chocolate that
small humans eat... and it has melted in the sun.
It would never have hatched into a kitten, Cat,"
Dog says gently.

"Oh," says Cat, orange fur turning red in
embarrassment. "Perhaps I should eat it then."

"No," says Dog. "You'll get very sick if you do.
Here. Take my dinner. I saved it for you," he says.

"Next time," Cat says, curling up against Dog, "I'll hatch it in the fridge. Anyway, what do you know?" she adds, eyes closing. "You're only a dog."

DID YOU KNOW THAT
CHOCOLATE IS BAD FOR PETS?

Chocolate smells and tastes yummy, doesn't it? But do you know that it's not good for our animal companions? Chocolate is safe for people, but it contains chemicals that are harmful to dogs and cats. Even small bites could make your pets very ill, and could result in seizures or cause their kidneys to fail.

So if your cat or dog asks for a bite of your chocolate, remember that it is poisonous for them, and don't give them any.

Oh, and make sure you stash those chocolate Easter eggs safely away, out of paw's reach!

Cataloging - in - Publication information:

Karthikeyan, Aparna
Cat's Egg / Aparna Karthikeyan; illustrated by Christine Kastl
p.32; color illustrations; 24.5 x 24 cm.

JUV000000 JUVENILE FICTION / General
JUV002000 JUVENILE FICTION / Animals / General
JUV002050 JUVENILE FICTION / Animals / Cats
JUV002070 JUVENILE FICTION / Animals / Dogs
JUV017020 JUVENILE FICTION / Holidays & Celebrations / Easter & Lent

ISBN 978-81-9365-422-4

Distributed in the United States by Consortium Book Sales & Distribution
www.cbsd.com